THE **BIG** TIME

RIHANNA

VALERIE BODDEN

CREATIVE EDUCATION

RIHANNA

TABLE OF CONTENTS

MEET RIHANNA

Fans scream and cheer inside a dark arena. Videos of Rihanna play on huge screens above a stage. One of the screens slides away. Rihanna is behind it, standing on a moving platform. She has a bright blue coat, pink shoes, and red hair. The crowd cheers louder as Rihanna starts to sing.

Rihanna (whose real name is Robyn Rihanna Fenty) is one of the biggest pop stars today. She is known for her dance, rhythm and blues, and hip-hop songs. Her albums sell millions of copies.

Rihanna likes to change her hair and clothing styles a lot

RIHANNA'S CHILDHOOD

Rihanna was born February 20, 1988, in Barbados, an island in the Caribbean Sea. Rihanna's parents divorced when she was 14. Rihanna and her two younger brothers lived with their mother.

Rihanna is one of the most famous people from Barbados

BARBADOS

GETTING INTO MUSIC

Before Rihanna's parents divorced, her dad ***abused*** her mom. Singing helped Rihanna deal with her worries. She sang at home in front of the mirror. She also sang at the beach and in ***clubs***.

Rihanna grew up in Bridgetown, the capital city of Barbados

In high school, Rihanna won a talent contest by singing a Mariah Carey song. She formed a band with two of her friends. She knew she wanted to be a pop star.

Rihanna sang her popular song "Pon de Replay" at a concert in August 2005

THE BIG TIME

When Rihanna was 15, she sang for an American ***music producer***. He brought her to the United States. In 2005, Rihanna's first album came out. It was called *Music of the Sun*.

Rihanna sang songs from her first album at concerts in late 2005

Rihanna made a new album almost every year after that. From 2005 to 2012, fans bought more than 37 million copies of her albums! She has won seven **Grammy Awards** for her music.

Rihanna and Jay-Z won a Grammy for their song "Umbrella"

OFF THE STAGE

Rihanna loves shoes. She has 1,500 pairs of them! In 2006, Rihanna started a ***charity*** called the Believe Foundation. It helps kids around the world get medical care and a good education.

Rihanna visited young patients at hospitals as part of her charity work

USS JOHN PAUL JONES
DDG-53

WHAT IS NEXT?

In 2012, Rihanna acted in her first movie, *Battleship*. She planned to make more movies in the future. And she hoped to someday start a ***fashion*** magazine or a clothing line. With so much going on, Rihanna will be busy for years to come!

Rihanna played the role of a U.S. Navy weapons specialist in Battleship

WHAT RIHANNA SAYS ABOUT ...

BEING A STAR

"This is what I was meant to do. This is what I dreamed of doing."

HER MOTHER

"She loved me unconditionally. She made us feel anything was possible and instilled in me such confidence."

LEAVING HOME

"When I left Barbados, I didn't look back. I wanted to do what I had to do, even if it meant moving to America."

GLOSSARY

abused hurt or treated badly

charity a group that works to help other people

clubs places where people go to hear music and dance

fashion a certain style or way of dressing

Grammy Awards the most famous music awards in the United States

music producer a person who helps a singer make and sell an album

READ MORE

Hibbert, Clare. *Pop Star*. Mankato, Minn.: Sea-to-Sea, 2012.

Tieck, Sarah. *Rihanna: Singing Sensation*. Minneapolis: Abdo, 2012.

WEBSITES

National Geographic Traveler: Barbados

http://travel.nationalgeographic.com/travel/countries/barbados-photos-traveler/

This site has lots of pictures of Rihanna's home country of Barbados.

Rihanna Biography

http://www.people.com/people/rihanna/

This site has information about Rihanna's life and many pictures, too.

INDEX

PUBLISHED BY Creative Education
P.O. Box 227, Mankato, Minnesota 56002
Creative Education is an imprint of The Creative Company
www.thecreativecompany.us

DESIGN AND PRODUCTION BY Christine Vanderbeek
ART DIRECTION BY Rita Marshall
PRINTED IN the United States of America

PHOTOGRAPHS BY Alamy (Photos 12), Corbis (John A. Angelillo, Kevork Djansezian/AP, Tim Mosenfelder), Getty Images (Scott Gries, Michael Hickey/WireImage, Stephen Lovekin/WireImage, Dan MacMedan/WireImage), iStockphoto (GYI NSEA, Pingebat, Cole Vineyard), Shutterstock (Darryl Brooks, Featureflash, s_bukley, Debby Wong)

LIBRARY OF CONGRESS CATALOGING-IN-PUBLICATION DATA
Bodden, Valerie.
Rihanna / Valerie Bodden.
p. cm. — (The big time)
Includes index.
Summary: An elementary introduction to the life, work, and popularity of Rihanna, a Barbados-born pop and hip-hop singer known for her colorful stage performances and such hit songs as "Umbrella."

ISBN 978-1-60818-479-8
1. Rihanna, 1988– —Juvenile literature. 2. Singers—Biography—Juvenile literature. I. Title.
ML3930.R44B63 2013
782.42164092—dc23 [B] 2013014411

9 8 7 6 5 4 3 2